HARPER & ROW, PUBLISHERS

Weekly Reader Books presents

WHO'S

AFRAID
OF THE DARK?

by Crosby Bonsall

An Early I CAN READ Book

*This book is a presentation of Weekly Reader Books.
Weekly Reader Books offers book clubs for children from
preschool through high school.*

For further information write to:
Weekly Reader Books
*4343 Equity Drive
Columbus, Ohio 43228*

Library of Congress Cataloging in Publication Data
Bonsall, Crosby Newell.
Who's afraid of the dark?

(An Early I can read book)
SUMMARY: A small boy projects his fear of the dark
onto his dog.
[1. Night—Fiction]   I. Title.
PZ7.B64265Wi   [E]   79-2700
ISBN 0-06-020598-9
ISBN 0-06-020599-7 lib. bdg.

I Can Read Book is a registered trademark of Harper & Row, Publishers, Inc.

Weekly Reader Books offers several exciting
card and activity programs. For information,
write to WEEKLY READER BOOKS, P.O. Box 16636,
Columbus, Ohio 43216.

I have told her it is silly.

I have told her I will protect her.

But Stella is still scared.

Stella is afraid of the dark.

For Elie and Jack

When we go to bed she shivers.

In the dark she shakes.

She sees big scary shapes.

10

She hears little scary sounds.

She hears *oooohs* and *boooos*.

I tell her it is only the wind.

But Stella is still scared.

She hears steps on the roof.

I tell her it is only the rain.

But she hides anyway.

Stella is not very smart, is she?

Yes, she is too!

16

Stella sounds sort of silly to me.

She is not!

She must be.

She's afraid of the dark.

That is not silly!

18

YOU said it was.

That's right.

Well, Stella IS silly.

19

But YOU are not silly.

Why don't you teach Stella

not to be afraid of the dark?

How?

Hold her and hug her.

Hang on to her in the dark.

Let her know you are there.

Take care of her!

After a while she will know.

After a while

she won't need you anymore.

23

Not ever?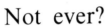

Only as a friend.

24

I will hold her

and hug her

tonight.

Don't be scared, Stella.

I will protect you.

I will take care of you.

29

30

31